Be careful as this small book ages,

Do not fold or tear the pages.

Treat it carefully as can be,

For this book belongs to me.

To my friend & mentor Victoria Rock,
who taught me more than I'll ever remember.

Copyright © 1999 by Sylvia Long.
All rights reserved.

Book design by Lucy Nielson and Susan Van Horn.
Typeset in Cantoria and Village.
The illustrations in this book were rendered in pen and ink with watercolor.
Manufactured in China.

Library of Congress Cataloging-in-Publication Data
Mother Goose. Selections.
Sylvia Long's Mother Goose / [illustrated] by Sylvia Long.
p. cm.
Summary: An illustrated collection of familiar nursery rhymes.
ISBN-13: 978-0-8118-2088-2
[1. Nursery rhymes. 2. Children's poetry. 3. Nursery rhymes.] I. Long, Sylvia, ill. II. Title.
PZ8.3.M85 1999
398.8—dc21   98-52311
CIP
AC

20 19 18 17 16 15 14

Chronicle Books LLC
680 Second Street, San Francisco, California 94107

www.chroniclekids.com

SYLVIA LONG'S
MOTHER GOOSE

chronicle books · san francisco

ARTIST'S NOTE

Mother Goose rhymes have such a long and deeply rooted tradition that I approached this project with some trepidation. After all, bookshelves are already filled with Mother Goose collections, many of them wonderful. I felt strongly that there was no point in doing another unless I could find ways to make it unique. So along with the most familiar rhymes, I have included quite a few less familiar ones. I have also tried to keep the classic qualities associated with Mother Goose while at the same time softening the more frightening images. Based on my own reactions as a child, I know that some of the imagery can be terrifying. It is not difficult for children to imagine what will happen when Humpty Dumpty or the rocking cradle hits the ground. In all but one case, "The Old Woman in the Shoe," I didn't feel justified in changing the words, but I tried to add a gentleness to the pictures. This doesn't mean that I have made the images "contemporary," but rather that I have tried to show that the rhymes can be interpreted in many different ways. Here, Peter Pumpkin-Eater's wife is quite cozy in her pumpkin shell. The baby in the cradle is a fledgling bird. And Humpty Dumpty, always a beloved character, may not be able to piece his shell together again, but that's not necessarily the end. A broken egg is not always a problem. Sometimes it's a duckling.

In addition, I have linked the pages visually to add another level of play, as well as a sense of cohesion to the collection. For instance, the spoon that runs away with the dish in "Hey, Diddle, Diddle" is the same spoon that Little

Miss Muffet later uses to eat her curds and whey. My hope is that readers will return to the book again and again, not only to hear the rhymes but also to pore over the images, finding new connections with each reading. When we make reading fun and surprising, we grow readers (and writers and artists). Many adults can look back and see that it was in these rhymes that they first found a love of language, rhythm and story. And for artists like myself, it is a place where many of us found images that remain vividly alive in our imaginations. Recited by heart, passed lovingly from parent to child, these verses — magical, musical, sometimes silly, sometimes wise — are part of our collective childhood.

This has been the most ambitious and challenging book project that I have been involved in, as well as the most fun. Now that I have had the privilege of helping with its creation, I hope that it will be enjoyed and loved by others.

Cackle, cackle, Mother Goose,
Have you any feathers loose?
Truly have I, pretty fellow,
Half enough to fill a pillow.
Here are quills, take one or two,
And down to make a bed for you.

Tweedle-dum and Tweedle-dee
Resolved to have a battle,
For Tweedle-dum said Tweedle-dee
Had spoiled his nice new rattle.

Just then flew by a monstrous crow,
As big as a tar barrel,
Which frightened both the heroes so
They quite forgot their quarrel.

Rock-a-bye, baby,
Your cradle is green;
Father's a nobleman;
Mother's a queen;
And Betty's a lady
And wears a gold ring,
And Johnny's a drummer
And drums for the king.

Once I saw a little bird
Come hop, hop, hop;
So I cried, "Little bird,
Will you stop, stop, stop?"
And was going to the window
To say "How do you do?"
But he shook his little tail,
And far away he flew.

Little Tommy Tittlemouse
Lived in a little house;
He caught fishes
in other men's ditches.

Daffy-Down-Dilly has now come to town
In her petticoat green and her bright yellow gown.

Humpty Dumpty sat on a wall;
Humpty Dumpty had a great fall.
All the king's horses, and all the king's men
Couldn't put Humpty together again.

Ring around the rosies,
A pocket full of posies.
Ashes, ashes,
We all fall down.

Mary, Mary, quite contrary,
How does your garden grow?
Silver bells and cockleshells,
And pretty maids all in a row.

Monday's child is fair of face,

Tuesday's child is full of grace,

Wednesday's child is full of woe,

Thursday's child has far to go,

Friday's child is loving and giving,

Saturday's child works hard for a living,

But the child that's born on Sabbath day
Is bonny and blithe, and good and gay.

There was a little girl who had a little curl
Right in the middle of her forehead;
When she was good, she was very, very good,
And when she was bad she was horrid.

Curly-locks, Curly-locks, wilt thou be mine?
Thou shalt not wash dishes, nor yet feed the swine;
But sit on a cushion, and sew a fine seam,
And feed upon strawberries, sugar, and cream!

Hey, diddle, diddle!
The cat and the fiddle,
The cow jumped over the moon;
The little dog laughed
To see such sport,
And the dish ran away
With the spoon.

Little Jack Horner
Sat in a corner,
Eating a Christmas pie.
He put in his thumb,
And pulled out a plum,
And said, "What a good boy am I!"

Little Miss Muffet
Sat on a tuffet,
Eating some curds and whey.
Along came a spider,
Who sat down beside her,
And frightened Miss Muffet away.

One, two, buckle my shoe;

Three, four, knock at the door;

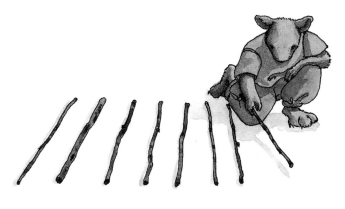

Five, six, pick up sticks;

Seven, eight, lay them straight;

Nine, ten, a good fat hen;

Eleven, twelve, dig and delve;

Thirteen, fourteen, maids a-courting;

Fifteen, sixteen, maids in the kitchen;

Seventeen, eighteen, maids a-waiting;

Nineteen, twenty, my plate's empty.

There was an old woman
Who lived in Dundee,
And in her back garden
There grew a plum tree;
The plums they grew rotten
Before they grew ripe,
And she sold them
Three farthings a pint.

Diddlety, diddlety, dumpty,
The cat ran up the plum tree;
Half a crown to fetch her down,
Diddlety, diddlety, dumpty.

Peter Piper picked a peck
Of pickled peppers;
A peck of pickled peppers
Peter Piper picked;
If Peter Piper picked a peck
Of pickled peppers,
Where's the peck of pickled peppers
Peter Piper picked?

Peter, Peter, pumpkin eater;
Had a wife, and couldn't keep her,
He put her in a pumpkin shell,
And there he kept her very well.

Bow, wow, wow!
Whose dog art thou?
Little Tom Tinker's dog,
Bow, wow, wow!

Old Mother Hubbard
Went to the cupboard
To get her poor dog a bone;
But when she got there
The cupboard was bare,
And so the poor dog had none.

31

Twinkle, twinkle, little star,
How I wonder what you are.
Up above the world so high,
Like a diamond in the sky.

When the blazing sun is gone,
When he nothing shines upon,
Then you show your little light,
Twinkle, twinkle, all the night.

Then the traveler in the dark
Thanks you for your tiny spark;
He could not see which way to go,
If you did not twinkle so.

In the dark blue sky you keep,
And often through my curtains peep,
For you never shut your eye,
Till the sun is in the sky.

As your bright and tiny spark
Lights the traveler in the dark,
Though I know not what you are,
Twinkle, twinkle, little star.

Dame Trot and her cat
Led a peaceable life,
When they were not troubled
With other folks' strife.

When Dame had her dinner
Pussy would wait,
And was sure to receive
A nice piece from her plate.

I love little pussy,
Her coat is so warm,
And if I don't hurt her
She'll do me no harm.

So I'll not pull her tail,
Nor drive her away,
But pussy and I
Very gently will play.

There were two birds sat upon a stone,
Fal de ral-al de ral-laddy.

One flew away, and then there was one,
Fal de ral-al de ral-laddy.

The other flew after, and then there was none,
Fal de ral-al de ral-laddy.

So the poor stone was left all alone,
Fal de ral-al de ral-laddy.

One of these little birds back again flew,
Fal de ral-al de ral-laddy.

The other came after, and then there were two,
Fal de ral-al de ral-laddy.

Says one to the other, "Pray how do you do?"
Fal de ral-al de ral-laddy.

"Very well, thank you, and pray how are you?"
Fal de ral-al de ral-laddy.

Hush-a-bye, baby, upon the tree top,
When the wind blows the cradle will rock;
When the bough breaks the cradle will fall,
And down will come baby, cradle and all.

Little Robin Red-breast
Sat upon a rail,
Niddle, naddle, went his head,
Wiggle, waggle, went his tail.

Baa, baa, black sheep, have you any wool?

Yes sir, yes sir, three bags full.

One for the master, and one for the dame,

And one for the little boy who lives down the lane.

Little Boy Blue, come blow your horn!
The sheep's in the meadow, the cow's in the corn.
Where is the boy that looks after the sheep?
Under the haystack, fast asleep!

Little Bo-Peep has lost her sheep,
And can't tell where to find them;
Leave them alone, and they'll come home,
Wagging their tails behind them.

Jack Spratt could eat no fat.
His wife could eat no lean;
So 'twixt them both they cleaned the cloth,
And licked the platter clean.

43

Hickory, dickory, dock; the mouse ran up the clock. The clock struck one, the mouse ran down, hickory, dickory, dock.

There's a neat little clock,
In the school room it stands,
And it points to the time
With its two little hands.

And may we, like the clock,
Keep a face clean and bright,
With hands ever ready
To do what is right.

Little Betty Blue
Lost her holiday shoe,
What shall little Betty do?
Give her another
To match the other,
And then she'll walk upon two.

Cobbler, cobbler, mend my shoe
Get it done by half past two;
Stitch it up, and stitch it down,
Make the finest shoes in town.

Lucy Locket lost her pocket,
Kitty Fisher found it;
There was not a penny in it,
But a ribbon 'round it.

Cock a doodle doo!

My dame has lost her shoe;

My master's lost his fiddling stick,

And knows not what to do!

Cock a doodle doo!

What is my dame to do?

Till master finds his fiddling stick,

She'll dance without her shoe.

Dance, little baby, dance up high!
Never mind, baby, mother is by.
Crow and caper, caper and crow,
There, little baby, there you go!
Up to the ceiling, down to the ground,
Backward and forward, round and round;
Dance, little baby and mother will sing,
With the merry chorale, ding, ding, ding!

Old King Cole was a merry old soul,
And a merry old soul was he;
He called for his pipe,
And he called for his bowl,
And he called for his fiddlers three.
And every fiddler, he had a fine fiddle,
And a very fine fiddle had he.
Oh, there's none so rare
As can compare
With King Cole
And his fiddlers three.

Pussycat, pussycat, where have you been?
I've been to London to see the Queen.
Pussycat, pussycat,
What did you there?
I frightened a little mouse
Under her chair.

The cock crows in the morn
To tell us to rise,
And he who lies late
Will never be wise:
For early to bed
And early to rise,
Is the way to be healthy
And wealthy and wise.

Diddle diddle dumpling, my son John
Went to bed with his breeches on,
One stocking off, and one stocking on;
Diddle diddle dumpling, my son John.

This is the way we wash our hands,

Wash our hands, wash our hands;

This is the way we wash our hands,

On a cold and frosty morning.

This is the way we wash our clothes,

Wash our clothes, wash our clothes;

This is the way we wash our clothes,

On a cold and frosty morning.

This is the way we go to school,

Go to school, go to school;

This is the way we go to school,

On a cold and frosty morning.

This is the way we come out of school,

Come out of school, come out of school;

This is the way we come out of school,

On a cold and frosty morning.

55

A was an angler,
Went out in a fog;
Who fished all the day,
And caught only a frog.

B was cook Betty,
A-baking a pie
With ten or twelve apples
All piled up high.

C was a custard
In a glass dish,
With as much cinnamon
As you could wish.

D was fat Dick,
Who did nothing but eat;
He would leave book and play
For a nice bit of meat.

E was an egg,
  In a basket with more,
Which Peggy would sell
  For a shilling a score.

F was a fox,
  So cunning and sly,
Who looked at the hen-roost—
  I need not say why.

G was a greyhound,
  As fleet as the wind;
In the race course
  Left all others behind.

H was a heron,
  Who lived near a pond;
Of gobbling the fishes
  He was wondrously fond.

I was the ice
   On which Billy would skate;
So up went his heels,
   And down went his pate.

J was Joe Jenkins,
   Who played on the fiddle;
He began twenty tunes,
   But left off in the middle.

K was a kitten,
   Who jumped at a cork,
And learned to eat mice
   Without plate, knife, or fork.

L was a lark,
   Who sang us a song,
And woke us sometimes
   When we slept too long.

M was Miss Molly
    Who turned in her toes,
And hung down her head
    Till her knees touched her nose.

N was a nosegay,
    Sprinkled with dew,
Pulled in the morning
    And presented to you.

O was an owl,
    Who looked wondrously wise;
But he's watching a mouse
    With his large round eyes.

P was a parrot,
    With feathers like gold,
Who talked just as much,
    And no more than he's told.

Q was the Queen
  Who governed the land,
And sat on a throne
  Very lofty and grand.

R was a raven
  Perched on an oak,
Who with a gruff voice
  Cried, "Croak, croak, croak!"

S was a stork
  With a very long bill,
Who swallowed down fishes
  And frogs to his fill.

T was a trumpeter
  Blowing his horn,
Who told us the news
  As we rose in the morn.

U was a unicorn,
  Who, as it is said,
Wore an ivory bodkin
  On his forehead.

V was a vulture
  Who ate a great deal,
Devouring a dog
  Or a cat as a meal.

W was a watchman
Who guarded the street,
Lest robbers or thieves
The good people should meet.

X was King Xerxes,
Who, if you don't know,
Reigned over Persia
A great while ago.

Y was the year
That was passing away,
And still growing shorter
Every day.

Z was a zebra,
Whom you've heard of before;
So here ends my rhyme
Till I find you some more.

A B C D E F G
H I J K L M N O P
Q R S T U V
W X Y and Z

Now I've said my A, B, Cs
Tell me what you think of me.

Rub-a-dub-dub,

Three men in a tub;

And who do you think they be?

The butcher, the baker,

The candlestick-maker;

Turn 'em out, knaves all three.

Three blind mice. Three blind mice.

See how they run! See how they run!

They all ran after the farmer's wife

Who cut off their tails with a carving knife.

Did you ever see such a thing in your life

As three blind mice?

Bow Wow

Mew Mew

Grunt Grunt

Squeak!

Bow-wow, says the dog;
Mew, mew, says the cat;
Grunt, grunt, goes the hog;
And squeak goes the rat.

Tu-whu, says the owl;
Caw, caw, says the crow;
Quack, quack, says the duck;
And what sparrows say, you know.

So with sparrows and owls,
With rats and with dogs,
With ducks and with crows,
With cats and with hogs,

A fine song I have made,
To please you, my dear;
And if it's well sung,
'Twill be charming to hear.

P olly, put the kettle on,

Polly, put the kettle on,

Polly, put the kettle on,

We'll all have tea.

S ukey, take it off again,

Sukey, take it off again,

Sukey, take it off again,

They're all gone away.

Pease porridge hot, pease porridge cold,

Pease porridge in the pot nine days old.

Some like it hot, some like it cold,

Some like it in the pot nine days old.

"To bed, to bed," says Sleepy-head;

"Let's stay awhile," says Slow.

"Put on the pan," says Greedy-Nan,

"We'll sup before we go."

There was an old woman
Who lived in a shoe.
She had so many children
She didn't know what to do.
So she gave them some broth,
With plenty of bread.
She kissed them all sweetly
And put them to bed.

Buttons, a farthing a pair!
Come, who will buy them of me?
They're round and sound and pretty,
And fit for the girls of the city.
Come, who will buy them of me?
Buttons, a farthing a pair!

There was a crooked man,
Who walked a crooked mile.
He found a crooked sixpence
Against a crooked stile;
He bought a crooked cat
Which caught a crooked mouse,
And they all lived together
In a little crooked house.

Sing a song of sixpence,
A pocket full of rye;
Four-and-twenty blackbirds
Baked in a pie.

When the pie was opened
The birds began to sing;
Wasn't that a dainty dish
To set before the king?

There were two blackbirds sitting on a hill.
One named Jack and the other named Jill.
Fly away, Jack! Fly away, Jill!
Come again, Jack! Come again, Jill!

Jack and Jill went up the hill
To fetch a pail of water;
Jack fell down and broke his crown,
And Jill came tumbling after.

"Yaup, yaup, yaup!"
Said the croaking voice of a frog;
"A rainy day
In the month of May,
And plenty of room in the bog."

"Yaup, yaup, yaup!"
Said the frog, as it hopped away;
"The insects feed
On the floating weed,
And I'm hungry for dinner today."

"Yaup, yaup, yaup!"
Said the frog, as it splashed about;
"Good neighbors all,
When you hear me call,
It is odd that you do not come out."

"Yaup, yaup, yaup!"
Said the frog; "It is charming weather;
We'll come and sup
When the moon is up,
And we'll all of us croak together."

Rain, rain, go away
Come again another day;
Little Johnny wants to play.

Wee Willie Winkie runs through the town,
Upstairs and downstairs, in his nightgown,
Tapping at the window, crying at the lock,
"Are the babes in their beds? For it's now eight o'clock."

Jack be nimble, Jack be quick, Jack jump over the candlestick.

Fiddle-de-dee, fiddle-de-dee,

The fly shall marry the bumblebee.

They went to the church, and married was she:

The fly has married the bumblebee.

Come take up your hats, and away let us haste,
To the Butterfly's Ball, and the Grasshopper's Feast.
The trumpeter, Gadfly, has summoned the crew,
And the revels are now only waiting for you.

Three little kittens they lost their mittens,
And they began to cry,
Oh, Mother dear, we sadly fear
That we have lost our mittens.
What! Lost your mittens, you naughty kittens!
Then you shall have no pie.
Mee-ow, mee-ow, mee-ow, mee-ow.
No, you shall have no pie.

The three little kittens they found their mittens,
And they began to cry,
Oh, Mother dear, see here, see here,
That we have found our mittens.
Put on your mittens, you silly kittens,
And you shall have some pie.
Purr-r, purr-r, purr-r, purr-r,
Oh, let us have some pie.

Ride a cock-horse
To Banbury Cross
To see what Tommy can buy.
A penny white loaf,
A penny white cake,
And a two-penny apple pie.

Simple Simon met a pieman
Going to the fair;
Said Simple Simon to the pieman,
"Let me taste your ware."

Said the pieman to Simple Simon,
"Show me first your penny."
Said Simple Simon to the pieman,
"Indeed I have not any."

To market, to market, to buy a fat pig,
Home again, home again, jiggety jig.
To market, to market, to buy a fat hog,
Home again, home again, jiggety jog.

Tom, Tom, the piper's son,
Stole a pig, and away he run;
The pig was eat, and Tom was beat,
And Tom ran crying down the street.

The north wind doth blow,
And we shall have snow,
And what will poor robin do then?
    Poor thing!

He'll sit in the barn
And keep himself warm,
And hide his head under his wing.
    Poor thing!

Come hither, sweet robin,
And be not afraid,
I would not hurt even a feather;
Come hither, sweet robin,
And pick up some bread,
To feed you in this very cold weather.
I don't mean to frighten you,
Poor little thing,
And pussycat is not behind me.
So hop about pretty,
And drop down your wing,
And pick up some crumbs,
And don't mind me.

Mary had a little lamb
With fleece as white as snow.
And everywhere that Mary went
The lamb was sure to go.

It followed her to school one day—
That was against the rule.
It made the children laugh and play
To see a lamb at school.

And so the teacher turned it out,
But still it lingered near,
And waited patiently about
Till Mary did appear.

"Why does the lamb love Mary so?"
The eager children cry.
"Why, Mary loves the lamb, you know!"
The teacher did reply.

This little piggy went to market,

This little piggy stayed home,

This little piggy had roast beef,

This little piggy had none,

This little piggy cried wee-wee-wee...

All the way home.

H ot-cross buns!
Hot-cross buns!
One a penny, two a penny,
Hot-cross buns!
If you have no daughters,
Give them to your sons.
One a penny, two a penny,
Hot-cross buns!

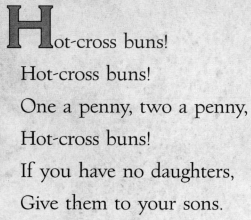

Pat-a-cake, pat-a-cake, baker's man,
Bake me a cake as fast as you can.
Roll it, and pat it, and mark it with B,
And put it in the oven for baby and me!

A robin and a robin's son
Once went to town to buy a bun.
They couldn't decide on plum or plain,
And so they went back home again.

I love you well, my little brother,
And you are fond of me;
Let us be kind to one another,
As brothers ought to be.

You shall learn to play with me,
And learn to use my toys;
And then I think that we shall be
Two happy little boys.

See saw, Margery Daw,
Jacky shall have a new master.
Jacky shall have but a penny a day,
Because he can't work any faster.

Come, my children, come away,
For the sun shines bright today;
Little children, come with me,
Birds and brooks and posies see;
Get your hats and come away,
For it is a pleasant day.

Everything is laughing, singing,
All the pretty flowers are springing;
See the kitten, full of fun,
Sporting in the brilliant sun;
Children too may sport and play,
For it is a pleasant day.

Bring the hoop, and bring the ball,
Come with happy faces all;
Let us make a merry ring,
Talk and laugh, and dance and sing.
Quickly, quickly, come away,
For it is a pleasant day.

Sleep, baby, sleep,
Our cottage vale is deep;
The little lamb is on the green,
With woolly fleece so soft and clean.
Sleep, baby, sleep.

Sleep, baby, sleep,
Down where the woodbines creep;
Be always like the lamb so mild,
A kind and sweet and gentle child.
Sleep, baby, sleep.

Bossy-cow, bossy-cow, where do you lie?
In the green meadow under the sky.

Billy-horse, billy-horse, where do you lie?
Out in the stable with nobody nigh.

Birdies bright, birdies sweet, where do you lie?
Up in the treetops—oh, ever so high!

Baby dear, baby love, where do you lie?
In my warm crib, with Mama close by.

Come to the window,
My baby, with me,
And look at the stars
That shine on the sea!
There are two little stars
That play at bo-peep
With two little fish
Far down in the deep,
And two little frogs
Cry "Neep, neep, neep."
I see a dear baby
That should be asleep.

INDEX OF FIRST LINES